Dear Parents:

Congratulations! Your child is taking the first steps on an exciting journey. The destination? Independent reading!

STEP INTO READING® will help your child get there. The program offers five steps to reading success. Each step includes fun stories and colorful art or photographs. In addition to original fiction and books with favorite characters, there are Step into Reading Non-Fiction Readers, Phonics Readers and Boxed Sets, Sticker Readers, and Comic Readers—a complete literacy program with something to interest every child.

Learning to Read, Step by Step!

Ready to Read **Preschool–Kindergarten**
• big type and easy words • rhyme and rhythm • picture clues
For children who know the alphabet and are eager to begin reading.

Reading with Help **Preschool–Grade 1**
• basic vocabulary • short sentences • simple stories
For children who recognize familiar words and sound out new words with help.

Reading on Your Own **Grades 1–3**
• engaging characters • easy-to-follow plots • popular topics
For children who are ready to read on their own.

Reading Paragraphs **Grades 2–3**
• challenging vocabulary • short paragraphs • exciting stories
For newly independent readers who read simple sentences with confidence.

Ready for Chapters **Grades 2–4**
• chapters • longer paragraphs • full-color art
For children who want to take the plunge into chapter books but still like colorful pictures.

STEP INTO READING® is designed to give every child a successful reading experience. The grade levels are only guides; children will progress through the steps at their own speed, developing confidence in their reading. The F&P Text Level on the back cover serves as another tool to help you choose the right book for your child.

Remember, a lifetime love of reading starts with a single step!

*To Greg, with love
and pink shirts always
—F.G.*

*For Wayne, Emily,
and Amelia
—E.U.*

Text copyright © 2017 by Frances Gilbert
Cover art and interior illustrations copyright © 2017 by Eren Unten

All rights reserved. Published in the United States by Random House Children's Books, a division of Penguin Random House LLC, New York.

Step into Reading, Random House, and the Random House colophon are registered trademarks of Penguin Random House LLC.

Visit us on the Web!
StepIntoReading.com
randomhousekids.com

Educators and librarians, for a variety of teaching tools, visit us at
RHTeachersLibrarians.com

Library of Congress Cataloging-in-Publication Data
Names: Gilbert, Frances, author. | Unten, Eren Blanquet, illustrator.
Title: I love pink! / Frances Gilbert, Eren Unten.
Description: New York : Random House, [2017] | Series: Step into reading. Step 1 | Summary: When her pets turn pink, a young girl has a hard time finding them in her pink bedroom.
Identifiers: LCCN 2015043655 (print) | LCCN 2016021308 (ebook) |
ISBN 978-1-101-93737-2 (trade pbk.) | ISBN 978-1-101-93738-9 (lib. bdg.) |
ISBN 978-1-101-93739-6 (ebook)
Subjects: | CYAC: Color—Fiction. | Pets—Fiction.
Classification: LCC PZ7.1.G547 Ial 2017 |
DDC [E]—dc23

Printed in the United States of America
10 9 8 7 6 5 4 3 2 1

This book has been officially leveled by using the F&P Text Level Gradient™ Leveling System.

STEP INTO READING®

STEP 1 READY TO READ

I Love Pink!

by Frances Gilbert
illustrated by Eren Unten

Random House 🏠 New York

My cat is orange.

My dog is black.

My hamster is brown.

But my room
is pink!

My bed is pink.

My pillows are pink.

My lamp is pink.

My desk is pink.

I love pink!

I do not like red.

I do not like blue.

I do not like green.

I only wear pink!

I wish my cat
were pink.

I wish my dog
were pink.

I wish my hamster
were pink.

Oops!
Now my pets
are pink.

I can not

find them!

Where is my cat?

Where is my dog?

Where is my hamster?

I wish my cat
were orange again!

A cat should not
be pink.

I wish my dog
were black again!

A dog should not be pink.

I wish my hamster
were brown again!

A hamster should not
be pink.

I still love pink.
But I love my cat
and my dog
and my hamster more!